SHARK SHOCK

Max's tongue began to tingle and there was that strange taste in his mouth. He coughed and spluttered, hanging on to the brass rail. Everyone's eyes turned to him.

'Max! What's the matter?' Mrs Murphy looked alarmed. Who should she help first? Molly in danger in the water, or Max choking on the yacht?

'J-just a sweet – went the wrong way!' Max gasped. One of the crew gave him a massive thump on the back, which made him choke even more.

'Thanks!' he wheezed. 'Got book – in cabin. Tells you – how to get away – from sharks . . .'

Max turned and ran to the back of the yacht, screaming in pain as two sharp rows of teeth forced themselves through his jaw, and another row behind them, and another row behind that . . .

One school holiday, Max and Molly go with their zoologist parents to Africa. Max develops a strange fever when he drinks from a stream and, after he's recovered, everything has changed – especially his attitude to animals.

The village healer tells him he now has a special skill: he's at one with the animals. But Max doesn't believe a word of it. At least, not until the first time his fingers tingle, his vision goes wobbly and his tongue gets thick and fuzzy . . .

Luckily, the effects never last more than a few hours, but that's still plenty of time for Max to get into some amazing scrapes, and to get first-hand experience of how the animal world sees humans.

For a boy who wants nothing more challenging than a computer game and a chocolate bar, life just got a whole lot more complicated . . .

BEASTLY!

SHARK SHOCK
Andy Baxter

Illustrations by Brian Williamson

EGMONT

Special thanks to:
Ann Ruffell, West Jesmond Primary School,
Maney Hill Primary School and
Courthouse Junior School

EGMONT
we bring stories to life

Shark Shock first published in Great Britain 2008
by Egmont UK Limited
239 Kensington High Street, London W8 6SA

Text & illustrations © 2008 Egmont UK Ltd
Text by Ann Ruffell
Illustrations by Brian Williamson

ISBN 978 1 4052 3936 3

1 3 5 7 9 10 8 6 4 2

A CIP catalogue record for this title is available
from the British Library

Typeset by Avon DataSet Ltd, Bidford on Avon, Warwickshire
Printed and bound in Great Britain by the CPI Group

'I liked the parts when Max transforms into different animals because it helps you to imagine how life is for those animals'
Billy, age 11

'I love the cliffhangers!'
James, age 9

'I'm going to read all the books!'
Luke, age 8

'I really loved this series – it's really cool and funny'
Oliver, age 10

'I wish I could transform like Max can!'
Connor, age 9

We want to hear what *you* think about *Beastly!* Visit:

www.beastlybooks.com

for loads of fearsomely good stuff to do!

BEASTLY!: The Characters

MAX MURPHY Chocolate fanatic and shape-shifter extraordinaire

Absent-minded Uncle Herbert looks after Max and his twin sister Molly during term time while their parents are away.

MOLLY MURPHY
Max's younger twin
(by ten minutes)
and protector of
his secret

Max longs for a normal family life,
but that's about as likely as his uncle
remembering which day of the week it is!

HERBERT SPLOTT
Could there be more
to Uncle Herbert
than meets the eye?

BEASTLY!: The Characters

Mr and Mrs Murphy are zoologists, so they're completely crazy about animals, and they're busy working on creating the best animal encyclopedia ever. Max thinks they're weird; who wants to stand around staring at sloths when you could be tucked up at home watching telly?

MR MURPHY AND MRS MURPHY
Very bright, but a little bit bonkers!
And completely clueless about
Max's secret...

PROFESSOR SLYNK
Mad, bad and dangerous
to know

And, as if all that didn't make Max's life tough
enough, his parents' sinister colleague Professor
Preston Slynk has found out his secret. Slynk's
miniature insect-robot spies are never far away . . .

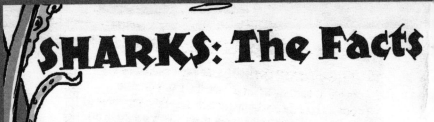

SHARKS: The Facts

They're nosy! Sharks can smell a drop of blood from around 4 kilometres away. In fact, two-thirds of a shark's brain is used for smelling!

Their ears aren't bad either! Sharks can hear sounds from thousands of metres away.

They're toothy! Sharks have the most powerful jaws on the planet. They can have up to 3,000 teeth at one time, arranged in rows. When one gets broken or damaged, another slides forwards to replace it. Some sharks may grow and use over 20,000 teeth in their lifetime!

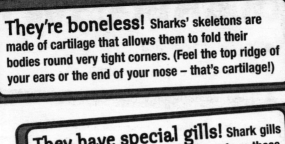

They're boneless! Sharks' skeletons are made of cartilage that allows them to fold their bodies round very tight corners. (Feel the top ridge of your ears or the end of your nose – that's cartilage!)

They have special gills! Shark gills (their breathing 'lungs') are different from those of other fish. Fish gills are covered, but shark gills are open, and are called 'gill slits'.

Their skin bites! Sharks' skin is covered with tiny little teeth. These are called 'denticles' and help protect them from injury.

They're not fussy eaters!
Most sharks are carnivores (meat-eaters) and a big meal can keep them going for two months. Strange items that have been found inside sharks include clothes, a drum, car number plates, a treasure chest and a bottle of wine!

COLOMBIA: The Facts

- It's in Latin America
- The capital city is Bogota
- The main language spoken is Spanish

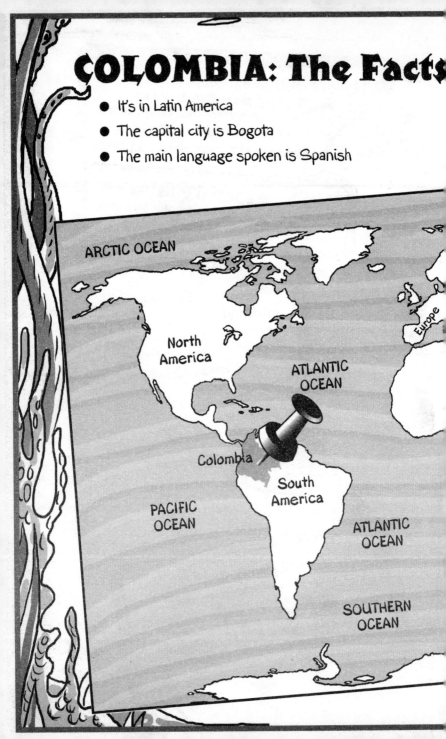

- Its weather is tropical on the coast, but cooler in the highlands
- Malpelo Island is off the coast of Colombia, and is home to lots of marine wildlife - including Galapagos sharks!

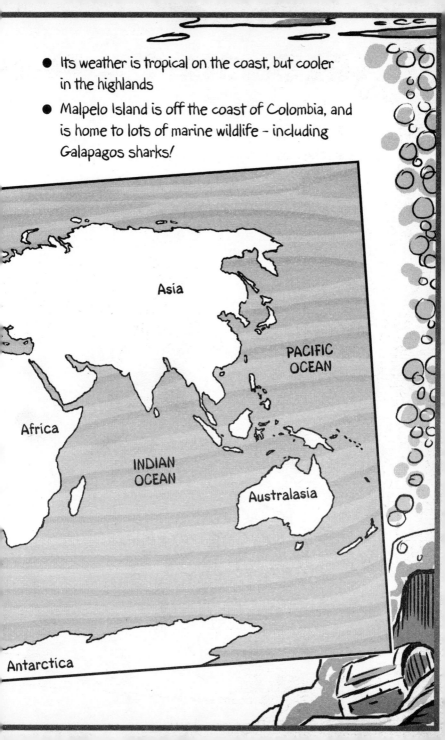

Contents

1. Party Pooper

'I can't believe you aren't excited!' Molly cried, as she and her brother made their way towards the school gates. 'Think about it! We could go snorkelling. Or scuba diving, even! Wouldn't that be brilliant?'

'Aren't snorkelling and scuba diving the same thing?' Max asked, although he didn't really care about the answer. It was the last day of school before the summer half term, which should have been cause for celebration. He'd planned to spend the whole holiday completing *Ecco the Dolphin* – a new console game he'd ordered – with his best friend, Jake. Unfortunately, his parents had other ideas, and he and his twin sister, Molly, had both been booked on a flight to . . . to . . .

'Where is it we're actually flying to again?'

'Cartagena in Colombia,' Molly sighed. 'How many times do I have to tell you?'

Max shrugged. 'Until I stop asking.'

'I think they play football there, too!' continued Molly. She was skipping now, the way she always did when she was excited. 'Maybe we can get a game!'

'Oh, you think so?' said Max, sarcastically. 'Whoopee!'

The fact was the only thing he'd hate more than playing a game of football was playing a game of football in Colombia. It wasn't that he had anything against Colombia in particular, it was just that he'd far rather be sitting at home watching a game of football on telly. Most of the time he hated having jet-setting parents. Today, though, he *really* hated it.

'Shame we'll have to miss the party at Samreen's house tomorrow, though,' Molly admitted. 'That would have been great!'

'I'd forgotten about that!' Max yelped. 'Oh, this just gets better and better doesn't it? So, I'm missing out on the party of the year *and* intensive computer sessions with Jake, for what? Two weeks at a . . . a . . .' he hesitated. 'What is it again?'

'It's Malpelo Island Flora and Fauna Sanctuary. We're catching a private plane there from Colombia,' tutted Molly. 'Try to pay attention!'

Max stopped in his tracks. 'Wait a minute,' he said, 'flora and fauna – that's plants and flowers and stuff, isn't it? Mum and Dad are zoologists;

they study animals, not plants! Why are we going to look at flowers?'

'Fauna means animals,' Molly explained, rolling her eyes. 'I thought everyone knew that!'

'I knew that, I was just testing to see if you did,' Max fibbed. 'Now come on. We're going to be late for school.'

Max dunked his last chip into his blob of tomato sauce then popped the whole thing in his mouth. All around him the canteen was filled with excited chatter about one thing and one thing only: Samreen's party.

'Shame you can't come,' said Jake, who was sitting directly across the table. Jake was Max's best friend and the only person, apart from Molly, he'd shared his secret with. 'Just about everyone is

going to be there. It's going to be awesome.'

'Yeah, well . . .' Max began.

'Samreen's mum and dad make the best food,' Jake drooled. 'There's usually loads and loads of it too. There's always tons left over!'

'Yes, thank you, I get the picture,' Max sighed. 'I feel bad enough already!'

'Oh, yeah, sorry,' Jake said. 'Still, you're going to Colombia!'

'Don't remind me!' said Max. 'Apparently they have lots of,' he shuddered as he said the next word, '*activities*.'

'What, like computer games?'

'*Physical* activities.'

'Oh, dear,' replied Jake. 'What are you going to do?'

'As little as possible, hopefully,' Max said. 'It's like they say, you can bring a boy to Colombia, but you can't make him scuba dive.'

'They don't say that,' Jake laughed.

'They will by the end of next week,' grinned Max.

'I hear you're not going to make it to my party,' said Samreen, as she sat down next to Jake. Molly walked up with her and sat next to her brother. Both girls put their dinner trays down on the table. Straight away, Max began to pick pieces of food from his sister's plate. 'That's a pity, it's going to be great!'

'So everyone keeps telling me,' Max nodded.

'My mum and dad have been cooking since Wednesday!' Samreen told him. 'We'll probably end up having to throw most of the food in the bin if you're not going to be there.'

'Really? That's a– hey, what's that supposed to mean?'

'She means you eat like a horse,' Molly explained. She jabbed her brother on the hand with her fork as he reached for one of her potatoes. 'Now leave my lunch alone!'

'Where is it you're going this time, anyway?' asked Samreen. Max shrugged and glanced at his sister.

'Colombia,' said Molly. 'It's going to be so great. We're going to go snorkelling, aren't we Max?'

'Well you might be,' Max replied. 'But if you

think I'm setting foot in the water you've got another thing coming!'

'Why not?' sneered an all-too-familiar voice from over Max's shoulder. 'I thought you'd be right at home down there with all those spineless little sea sponges!'

The twins turned and looked up into the grinning face of Stewart Staines. Stewart spent break times going round the school making the lives of other kids miserable. Max sighed. Was it his turn again so soon?

'All right, Brain Strain?' Max nodded.

'I told you,' the bully seethed, 'never call me that!'

'Sorry,' smirked Max, 'it must've slipped my mind.'

'Did someone mention a party?' asked Brain Strain hopefully. Samreen sighed. She hadn't invited Stewart. 'It's a real shame you're going to

miss it.' Stewart continued. 'I'm sure it'll be much more fun than mucking around with a load of stinking sea sponges!' He leaned down so his face was next to Max's. 'Apparently they're the smelliest creatures in the sea. Nothing else that lives down there will even go near them, that's how disgusting they are!'

'Why are you going on about sea sponges?' asked Max.

'You get them around Colombia,' said Stewart, trying his best to sound intelligent. 'Saw it in a documentary last night.'

'Right,' snorted Max. 'And when you say "documentary" do you in fact mean "cartoon"?'

Brain Strain opened his mouth to answer, but the bell rang for the end of lunch and stopped him in his tracks.

'We'll finish this later, Murphy,' he spat, before storming off out of the dinner hall.

'See you later,' said Molly to Max, as she and Samreen got up from the table. Jake began to move, but Max held his arm.

'D'you know if Brain Strain's right?' he asked. 'About sea sponges?'

'No idea, why?'

'I might change into one!'

'Oh, yeah,' Jake winced. 'That would be horrible.'

Max nodded. Changing into a sea sponge *would* be horrible, and there was no way of knowing if it was going to happen. He didn't know how his transformations worked. All he could do was wait and see.

The smelliest creature in the sea, he *thought. Won't that be just my luck?*

2. Spanish Doubloons

'Why don't they make snorkels fold up so you can get them in your backpack?' Molly was chattering as they walked home from school. 'If I put it into my big case it's sure to go somewhere really stupid – like China – by accident, but it just won't fit into my cabin baggage.'

'What?' said Max. He wasn't listening. His mind was still worrying about turning into a sea sponge. 'Do you think I'll have lots of little animals swimming in and out of my spaces? Or bits of grit getting stuck in me?'

Molly stared at him. 'Spaces? What spaces?'

'You know – the holes all through them. Sea sponges – what Brain Strain was on about.'

'You don't want to listen to him,' said Molly fiercely. 'Trust him to come up with something disgusting like that. Anyway, you won't turn into a sponge.'

'You don't know what I'll turn into,' gloomed Max. '*I* don't know what I'll turn into.'

He kicked a neat front gate that cut off a neat front garden from the footpath. There were so many really nasty things he might transform into – a slug, for instance. He didn't think he could cope with being a slug.

'Ooh, I mustn't forget to pack my football boots!' Molly raced ahead of Max, to where Uncle Herbert's rambling, ramshackle Victorian house lurked, next to the row of tidy modern houses. He heard her faintly as she disappeared down the shady drive. 'How many kilos am I allowed to take? I'll *never* get everything in!'

As Max pushed the heavy front door his spirits lifted a little. His new computer game was waiting for him, and Jake would be over later to play it with him. With any luck they should get a few hours in before he had to get on the plane to Cartagena.

But only a few hours! His face fell again. Couldn't his parents just for once let him have a proper half-term holiday at home with his mates?

'Face as long as a fiddle,' commented Uncle Herbert, suddenly appearing in front of him and making Max jump. 'What's the matter, old chap?'

'Oh, I just wanted to play with my new game and there won't be much time.' No point telling his absent-minded uncle more than that – he'd only ask again in five minutes, by which time Max hoped he would be upstairs switching on his console.

'Colombia,' said his uncle in a dreamy voice. The daily paper with a half-finished crossword dangled from his hand. 'Such an exciting place!'

Max looked at him curiously. Excitement didn't seem part of Uncle Herbert's life. Not the one he knew anyway.

'Particularly the waters around it,' his uncle went on. 'Malpelo Island is pretty uninhabited, but underwater you'll love it. Manta rays; Galapagos sharks; hammerhead sharks in great schools . . .'

'Don't tell me,' interrupted Max, 'the little ones go to plaice school!'

Uncle Herbert looked a bit blank.

'Play school – *plaice* school,' said Max helpfully.

'Ha, ha!' guffawed Uncle Herbert. 'I must write that one down.' He fumbled in his pocket for a pen and several torn scraps of paper flew out. 'And it's not just the fish – you must look out for wrecks.'

'Wrecks?' That was the last thing Max wanted to know about. He was always a bit queasy on boats anyway. He didn't want to end up fathoms down on the sea floor just because Mum and Dad wanted to add a rare jellyfish to their animal encyclopedia. And he wasn't sure he wanted to get too close to hammerhead sharks.

'Old wrecks,' said Uncle Herbert mysteriously. 'When the Spanish came to conquer the new world of South America, several of their galleons went under. Those that didn't get attacked by pirates, that is. Treacherous coast. Terrible storms.' He looked round as if someone might be listening, and bent his head down to Max's ear. 'Spanish gold and treasure!'

'Yeah, yeah,' said Max, itching to go up to his room. 'Look, I'd better go and pack.'

Uncle Herbert gave him an unexpectedly sharp look. 'You'll be spending most of your time on a boat,' he snapped. 'Like I said, there's not much on the island except boobies.' Max's eyebrows shot up. 'No, they're not stupid people, they're birds. All the really good stuff's in the sea. When she phoned last night, your mother said you'd be joining them on a friend's yacht. A luxury yacht. So I wondered if you could look out for the *Mala Noche* for me.'

'The Maller Nochay?'

'It means "Bad Night". A pirate ship. It must have given lots of sailors really bad nights in its day! I explored it once.' Uncle Herbert's blue eyes went dreamy. 'A long time ago. A very, very long time ago,' he added to himself. He looked at Max as if he wanted to say more, then changed his mind. 'Why are dolphins cleverer than humans?'

'I don't know, why are they?' said Max.

'Because they can train people to stand on the side of a pool and feed them fish!' chortled his uncle. 'Don't go away.'

And with that, he disappeared round a corner of the kitchen and into a secret passage. Max and Molly had only found the passage a month before, even though they'd been coming to Uncle Herbert's house for years.

Max tapped the side of his forehead with a finger. *Completely mad*, he said to himself. But just as he was about to go upstairs to his room — and the computer game — Uncle Herbert came bouncing back out of what looked like part of the panelling.

'Look!' he said triumphantly.

In his hand was a dull, round coin.

'Let me guess. An old penny,' said Max, deeply unimpressed.

Uncle Herbert rubbed it with his sleeve and it began to gleam with a warm, golden glow. It was roughly circular, and decorated with castles and what looked like lions standing on their rear legs. 'A Spanish doubloon,' said Uncle Herbert in a trembling whisper. 'And there were more. Chests full of them!'

Amazed, Max put his hand out to touch it. 'Brilliant!' he breathed.

'Here,' said Uncle Herbert. 'You can take it with you. You never know, it may bring you good luck!'

Max wondered whether they'd be able to go and explore the wrecks. Perhaps scuba diving wouldn't be such a bad thing after all, if he could be bothered to learn how. It couldn't be that hard, surely?

But he would pack his games console, just in case.

'Got it all in!' Molly jumped down the last three steps of the stairs triumphantly. 'What's for supper, Uncle Herbert?'

'Ah – now, I was watching a TV programme and they said to try mushy peas with raspberry jam. So I've done them on toast.'

'Er – can I have them separately?' said Max. 'Hey, Moll – we're going on a luxury yacht.'

'Cool,' said Molly. 'I've got my snorkel in my case. Whose yacht is it?'

Uncle Herbert scratched his head. 'Slime? Was that his name? No – Slynk. Yes, Professor Preston Slynk. "Slynk" rhymes with "Stink" – yes, that's how I remembered it. I wonder if I could get a crossword clue out of that?'

He pulled out another of his scraps of paper and pottered away to the kitchen without noticing the expressions on the twins' faces.

'Professor Stink!' hissed Molly. 'I don't believe it!'

Professor Preston Slynk was the twins' least favourite person. He was the only person, besides Molly and Jake, who knew about Max's strange transformations. If Slynk could find out how Max changed into an animal he might be able to do it himself. And then he could rule the animal kingdom – just think how many more insects there are than people!

Not surprisingly, Max wasn't keen for Slynk to experiment on him. From the look on his face, you'd think he'd already eaten his uncle's foul supper with some raw jellyfish relish on the side.

'Oh, nooo!' he cried. 'And I'd begun to think we were going to have a trouble-free trip for a change. If it's *his* yacht we'll *never* get away from him!'

3. Desperate Dolphin

'Weren't we lucky?' chirped Mrs Murphy, as soon as her children stepped on to the gleaming white boat. 'We'd only started talking about this trip when Preston came up with the idea we should join him on his yacht!'

'Yeah, great, Mum,' mumbled Max, eyeing Slynk suspiciously. Molly clutched her case tightly as Slynk tried to take it from her. No *way* was she going to let him get his podgy mitts on her snorkel!

The Professor rubbed his sweaty hands together and beamed all over his chubby face.

'*So* nice to see you again, Max. And you too, Molly! I'm really pleased you could find the time to come and join us here on my yacht.'

He waved his hands expansively at the smart deck and gleaming brass.

'I bet you are!' muttered Max, but not so that

his mother could hear.

'Would you like to show them their cabins, Preston?' said the twins' mum. She ran her fingers distractedly through her mop of blonde hair. 'Manfred saw a school of hammerhead sharks this morning. We're going to go diving and try to get pictures of them.'

'Of course. You carry on,' said Slynk heartily. But as soon as she had gone he bent his face down to Max's level. Not that he had to bend very far! The professor was rather sensitive about his height – or lack of it.

'This time, little boy, you won't be able to get away so easily!' he hissed unpleasantly. 'I shall be watching you very closely.'

'What will you be watching?' said Max innocently. 'I've brought my new computer game, *Ecco the Dolphin*. Do you want to watch me play?'

'You might even learn something,' snapped

Molly. She dragged her case across the shining deck leaving scratch marks from the corner where a wheel had fallen off.

Max sniggered and dragged his after her. Unfortunately the wheels on his case worked perfectly.

'Let me show you to your cabins,' said Slynk smoothly, rushing up behind them with hatred glistening in his eyes.

Molly knocked on Max's door after quickly stowing away her clothes. Her snorkel and mask dangled from her right hand.

'Look – we can see right out over the sea from here!'

There was a little passageway between his window and the railing on the sides of the yacht.

The sea seemed to be moving up and down in a most unpleasant way. Max turned away and tried to think of something else. But all that would come into his head were shipwrecks.

Everything had been such a rush that he didn't get a chance to show Molly Uncle Herbert's Spanish doubloon. He told her about the wreck beneath them though, while he carefully unpacked his computer console and threw his clothes on to the floor.

'And it's called the *Mala Noche*,' he said, pronouncing the words slowly.

'Cool!' said Molly. 'Let's ask Mum and Dad if we can visit it!'

'Later,' said Max. 'Just now I'm going to play my computer game.'

'I'm going swimming off the side of the boat,' said Molly. 'You can watch me.'

'Might do,' said Max with a shudder.

But Max couldn't concentrate on his game, because people kept walking past his window. He saw Molly jump off the side and begin to swim strongly away from the boat. At first he thought he'd been playing too much of his *Ecco* game, for suddenly he saw a fin and a rounded, glistening back. But it was real. A friendly, inquisitive dolphin had swum up to Molly and started playing with her. Max stared through the glass, letting the console fall from his hands.

Molly turned on to her back and kicked her feet. The dolphin plunged into the water with a great splash, then suddenly rose out again in a beautiful arc of spray.

'Oh, fantastic!' shouted Molly. She turned on to her front and swam with the creature. It slowed down to keep to her pace, then shot off again, leaping in the air before slapping down into the waves. Molly giggled. Her mouth filled with water from the dolphin wave. She spluttered and giggled again. 'Hey, look at me! Look at this dolphin!' she yelled.

Another shadow went by Max's window. It was Professor Slynk.

Max crept to the side of the window so that Slynk couldn't see him.

The professor was watching Molly and her sea playmate. He was clutching something in his podgy right hand. And his eyes were greedily following the antics of the dolphin.

'He thinks it's me!' chortled Max. He grinned as he watched his enemy leaning over the railings to get a better view. *Pity we can't shove him overboard to join in the fun!* he thought. Max slipped on his swimming trunks. He was trying to dream up a good way of surprising Slynk. A tap on the shoulder? Or should he just dive overboard?

Suddenly, the dolphin gave a high-pitched screech. Molly turned, startled. The dolphin looked at her as if to say, *Why are you doing this to me?* It clattered its teeth angrily.

Slynk was leaning over the side of the boat with an evil grin on his face. He had sent one of his nasty little robot insects into the dolphin's side with a tranquilliser dart! Molly didn't see the tiny box with legs dangling from the dolphin's side. The dart wasn't doing its job properly. The dolphin was anything but tranquillised! It gave Molly another thump with its muscular side. She saw the dolphin wince with pain.

'Oh, no!' she breathed. 'Sorry, dolphin – but I didn't hurt you.'

But how can you explain that to an injured dolphin? Molly kept on trying to soothe it and reassure it, but the dolphin bumped into her, shoving her menacingly with more of its high-pitched screams.

'What's happened?' Mr Murphy's deep voice called.

'Dad! The dolphin's injured and it thinks I've hurt it!' yelled Molly.

'We'll throw you a lifebelt!' Mr Murphy shouted back, as a member of the crew tried to pull one off its hooks.

'I'm *fine*!' roared Molly. 'Help the dolphin!'

'Yes, get the dolphin out!' shouted Slynk excitedly. He was hopping with anticipation, trying to stop people from pulling Molly out of the sea so that he could get at the dolphin.

Mrs Murphy came flying out. 'Darling! Are you all right? Try to keep still. They won't attack if you keep still!'

'It won't attack!' bawled Slynk. 'It knows it's . . .'

'Knows what?' said Max into his ear.

'Wha– what?' sputtered Slynk, reeling. 'How are you . . .? I mean, why are you . . .?'

'Here?' said Max innocently. 'You invited me, Professor. Remember?'

How could Max be on the boat? He was – surely he was – down there in the water, with his sister! Slynk leaned over the railing to see the dolphin barging at Molly.

He turned back with a snarl, but Max was still standing on the deck, hands on hips, laughing.

'I'll . . . I'll *get* you!' he rasped.

'Good try,' said Max. 'Pity it isn't me, isn't it?'

'I, er . . .' the professor began, then started to skulk off.

Max looked down over the railing. Molly yelled up at him. 'Max! *Do* something!'

Max's smile slipped from his face as he realised Molly was starting to really get frightened. He

hadn't seen just how hard the dolphin was barging at his sister, slapping its smooth sides against her.

On board everyone was shouting, yelling advice at each other. Some spoke in English, some in South-American Spanish. The sailor trying to free the lifebelt had somehow jammed it instead.

Suddenly, Mrs Murphy let out a scream.

Attracted by the noise from the yacht and the frantic splashing of the dolphin, a large Galapagos shark was lazily circling the scene.

4. Armed to the Teeth

Everyone followed Mrs Murphy's gaze and her pointing finger.

'*Shark*! Someone save Molly!' she choked.

The sinister black fin cruised slowly towards the frantic dolphin.

'It's a Galapagos shark,' she screeched. 'We've got to get her out – they attack humans!'

'Keep close to the dolphin!' Mr Murphy shouted to Molly. 'Sharks don't attack dolphins! Don't panic – I'm coming to get you out!'

There was a frantic bustle on the boat as people threw down rope ladders and tried to find scuba-diving equipment, but nobody seemed to know the right thing to do. The twins' dad stripped off his shirt but their mum grabbed his arm. 'There are plenty of sailors here prepared to go. I don't want to risk you too!' she panicked.

The shark was waiting for the right time. There was no hurry. There were no other sharks nearby to share its meal with. It needed to feel the vibrations in the water so that it knew where to strike to get its prey.

The captain of Slynk's yacht had shrugged off his uniform down to swimming shorts and now dived cleanly into the rippling waves. He called back to his crew in Spanish. The crew scuttled about the boat, obviously looking for something.

But Max was starting to feel the now familiar sensations that meant a transformation was coming on. His tongue began to tingle and there was that strange taste in his mouth.

His heart thumped as if he had been running very fast for a long time. He tried to pant, but he was finding it hard to breathe.

'Dad, I . . .' he choked. He had to get out of sight! What was he turning into?

'Not now, Max!' commanded his dad. For once, the absent-minded professor was snapping into action. His daughter was in danger and somehow they had to save her.

Max coughed and spluttered, hanging on to the brass rail. Everyone's eyes turned to him.

'Max! What's the matter?' Mrs Murphy looked alarmed. Who should she help first? Molly in danger in the water, or Max choking on the yacht?

Max took as deep a lungful of air as he could, but his windpipe seemed to be shrinking.

'J-just a sweet – went the wrong way!' he gasped.

One of the crew gave Max a massive thump on the back, which made him choke even more.

'Thanks!' he wheezed. 'Dad! Got book – in cabin. Tells you – how to get away – from sharks . . .'

Hoping everyone would understand what he was saying, Max turned and ran to the back of the yacht, tearing off his swimming trunks as he went. His head felt huge, his nose seemed to have forced itself forward so far that he nearly toppled over, and somehow his mouth and teeth were sliding underneath his face. There wasn't room in his mouth! He screamed in pain as two sharp rows of teeth forced themselves through his jaw, and another row behind them, and another row behind that . . .

Max felt his skin was crawling with a million ants as tiny, sharp denticles burst through it, making it rough as a cat's tongue. His back arched as a huge dorsal fin thrust itself out like a prehistoric sail. It hurt furiously.

The last few metres on deck were agony. Max's legs seemed to be fused together. Trying to use his feet to run felt as if he was splitting himself in half.

He jumped overboard clumsily. His arms had somehow disappeared and were now flapping fins. He felt his feet flatten and widen as he hit the water.

Suddenly, he stopped spluttering. He tried to breathe, but instead of his nostrils sucking in air,

he could feel vents opening in the sides of his neck.

Phew! thought Max. He started to calm down as water streamed over his gills. Wonderful oxygen filtered through them into his blood. His amazing new streamlined body powered him through the water like a torpedo. His bones seemed to have changed too. They were no longer stiff human bones, but strong, flexible cartilage. Max couldn't be sure, but he suspected he'd turned into a rather fine specimen of a Galapagos shark. His body bent almost in half as his fins steered him round towards the front of the yacht where the other shark was stalking his twin.

Everyone was hanging over the rail again, watching the captain's dark figure as the shark slowly circled the boat. He was still quite a long way from Molly and the dolphin, and it was only a matter of time before the shark struck.

'Try not to move!' shrieked Mr Murphy, as the

crew continued fumbling about on deck. 'Just remember, they won't attack if you don't move!' At least he knew Molly could be trusted to do the right thing.

The dolphin seemed to know about this too. It had frozen as if it had just been doused in quick-drying concrete. Molly tried to keep still, but she had to stay afloat. She was treading water nervously, trying to make her movements as small as possible.

'There's two of them!' someone shouted.

Molly's shriek could have woken the dead.

'Keep still!' bawled the twins' dad. 'Don't let it know you might be something to eat!'

Oh, great — just what you want to tell someone who's about to be chomped up by a shark! thought Max, as he powered his way towards the other shark. It recognised another of its kind, but that didn't make it friendly. It began to move towards Max, thrashing its tail in warning.

Yeah, but I'm bigger than you. Max sent the thought waves over to the monster fish, feeling the strength of his own muscles rippling down his body. He could sense the other shark near him. It seemed puzzled. It snapped as Max whooshed by and he felt a tiny graze on his thick shark skin.

This was getting scary. Did the other shark know he was really human? Or was this what sharks did for fun?

Suddenly, Max's animal self understood completely. He sped towards the real shark, jaws wide, as big and threatening as he could be. The real shark did a jack-knife turn, twisting its body away from Max.

Max pursued it, snapping his fearsome teeth. He raced through the blue water, chasing his rival away. Giant schools of striped angelfish separated, then gathered together again in a cloud after he had passed. Shoals of tiny silvery fish panicked

and swooped into dark forests of frondy seaweed. A huge manta ray cruised above him, saw him and hastily swam off.

The other Galapagos shark was gone. It knew who was boss in this part of the ocean. Max began to feel rather important, and snapped lazily at a tuna, which came rather closer than it meant to. He swerved his massive body round to go back and snatch at it. He was hungry. He could smell the blood from the dart that had pierced the dolphin's side and, though he didn't want to eat dolphin, the taste of blood made him ravenous.

Max knew about humans: his shark brain told him they had too many bones. He would only eat one of them if there was nothing else. But tuna were sweet, their flesh smooth and easy to rip apart. How many more of them were swimming about in the water? If he could find a shoal of tuna he could gorge for days. But a single one, with none of its friends to protect it, would be easier to stalk and catch.

The wounded dolphin was still butting Molly. The noise made Max-the-shark all excited. He wanted to kill, and kill fast!

It took Max-the-boy all his energy and focus to fight against his shark instinct and go near the splashing humans without attacking them.

He came up near the surface, his dorsal fin slicing the waves. He could smell the yacht and hear the still-frantic cries from the people on board. They were trying to lower something down to the captain – and making a lot of noise about it.

Honestly, don't they know that making all that racket will only make things worse? Max thought, as he barrelled his way towards the front of the yacht.

The dolphin was still there, trying to push Molly into the side of the boat. Max rammed himself against it, and the animal sped away in terror, trying to escape from the predator's terrifying jaws.

But the jolt he gave the dolphin knocked something away from its smooth side. Something he had seen before. He swam closer and saw it properly. A familiar little dart, with a tiny insect-like robot dangling from it. The dart hadn't gone right in, but it must have really irritated the dolphin. So *that's* what had happened to turn a friendly creature into a furious one.

A robotic spy that could only have come from one person.

Slynk!

If one of those came his way, Max would be in deadly danger. Slynk would be able to track him wherever he went.

5. Snap to It!

'Don't you dare come near me! I'll bash you on the nose!' screeched Molly. Max tried to grin. Best keep away from her until she knew who he was. Molly could throw a prize punch when she wanted!

His mouth gaped to show rows of sharp teeth. Molly screamed even louder.

'Moll, it's me!' he shouted, but he couldn't make words with his mouth — trying to only made his jaws snap crazily.

He could hear everyone else on the yacht shouting themselves hoarse. The captain was clambering into a small, inflatable boat. He had something long and pointed in his hand. A harpoon! Oh, no! The only reason he hadn't thrown it yet was because Molly was in the way!

It was time to get away. But first Max had to try and make Molly understand who he was.

He powered his body round so that he was opposite her red, screeching face, and winked slowly.

Instead of the scary, dark, shark eyes she was expecting, Molly was looking straight into Max's blue ones. 'Oh!' spluttered Molly. 'Oh – it's you!' She lowered her fist and splashed her arm back into the water, waving both hands to keep herself afloat. She pushed up her mask to the top of her head and spat out the snorkel. 'You'd better get away,' she gasped. 'When I get back on board I'll tell them you're in your cabin playing your dolphin game.'

Good old Molly! As soon as she'd stopped being scared to bits she was making sure he was OK. Max lifted his jaws to laugh, but to everyone on the yacht it seemed as if he was about to strike the girl in the water. They let out a combined shriek.

Max could see the captain steadying his harpoon, ready to fire.

Max wanted to tell Molly about the robotic dart that had got stuck in the dolphin's side, but he had only his fins to waggle. When he got back to being a boy again, Max decided, he'd learn sign language.

But trying to do any kind of signing with his fins was difficult. If he moved them one way he found himself swimming past Molly, and if he moved them the other way he headed straight for the harpoon. Desperate, he swam behind Molly to get away from the deadly weapon.

Suddenly, he saw it again; the tiny robot box

with the dart that had fallen out of the dolphin's side. He was sure Molly hadn't spotted it. He needed to tell her why the dolphin had behaved so badly to her. Pushing the tiny machine with his nose, he managed to get it near enough to Molly for her to see.

'Slynk!' he could hear her furious bellow even over the noise of the passengers in the yacht. 'That slimy stinker!' She picked it out of the water to

show Max. She knew exactly what he was trying to tell her.

'Look, it's friendly!' shouted one of the crew on the boat. 'Don't shoot it!'

The captain held the harpoon over his shoulder uncertainly.

'That's quite amazing!' said Mr Murphy. 'I've never seen a friendly shark before – not in the wild.'

'And an aggressive dolphin,' agreed Mrs Murphy.

'Perhaps this shark's escaped from a sea-life zoo,' said Slynk, his eyes glaring. 'We should capture it and get it put back where it belongs. You can't trust tamed predators – you never know when they might revert to the wild and attack again.'

'Darling, are you all right?' the twins' mum called down to Molly. 'We'll get you out of there straight away! Swim over to the captain's boat.'

'I'm fine!' bawled Molly. 'It was that dolphin. It got something stuck in its side.'

'Strange behaviour for animals in this part of the ocean,' Slynk was saying. 'Maybe there's something in the water that affects them. We need to find out. Have you got a tranquilliser dart, Manfred?'

You know full well he has, but you're not going to let on you've got some too, thought Max whipping his tail round with a great rush of spray. He needed to get away before his parents decided to experiment on him too!

Molly was safe now, so he could go exploring for a bit – so long as he got back in time. He'd have to be careful not to stay out there too long and be miles away from the yacht when he transformed back to a boy.

'Noooo!' He could just hear Molly yelling as he sped through the blue water. 'Leave it alone!'

So Slynk got his way, thought Max grimly. He dived deep down into the water, well out of the way of any tranquilliser darts.

On previous trips, Molly had tried to tell Max what she'd seen when she was snorkelling, but he'd never been interested enough to listen properly. He hadn't realised that the ocean floor was as bumpy as the land above. Great mountains rose from the depths with funny hairy things on them. He piloted himself through the canyons and gorges as if he were flying through the air and stared at some of the creatures glued to the rocks. The hairy things seemed to be growing out of part of the rock. And there were other jelly-like things, which waved pink tentacles at him.

His keen shark eyes saw brilliant colours.

Bright red and yellow fish peered out of the coral mountains, but shot back when they saw him coming. Small electric-blue fish burst into fans of colour as his shadow fell on them. Shoals of snappers and jacks seemed to mock him with their numbers, then flew away in great spinning clouds.

In the blue distance Max saw his cousins, a vast school of hammerhead sharks, forming and re-forming. Their strange axe-like heads made it look as though they were digging up everything in front of them like an army of labourers. Max's shark instincts knew they were bad news. They might be relatives, but they were likely to attack him if he got too near.

But away from the hammerheads Max felt like a king. All the other fish kept a respectful distance from him. Most of all he enjoyed thrusting his head up out of the water when he saw the shadows of boats above him. Nobody ignored him. They either pointed and shouted, 'Ooh! Shark! Wow, isn't it *big*!' as his dorsal fin broke the surface, or they screamed and ran about the decks, crashing into each other.

There was a huge trench ahead of him, dark and scary. He felt as if the steep coral sides were pressing in on him as he dived deeper. There were not so many fish here, unless they were hiding in the cracks. Then a big moray eel suddenly thrust its head out of a hole in the coral and snapped at him. Max swerved. *Hey, you're supposed to be scared of me*, he complained to himself. *Do morays eat sharks?* he thought. *Better keep out of its way, just in case.*

Max was feeling hungry again – shark hungry. A turtle that had swum down out of its depth passed by and he could almost feel the delicious crunch of underbelly in his teeth. But the boy part of him fought to resist the temptation to rush at the creature with open jaws.

As he fought against the killer instinct, he saw

another cloudy form. It looked spiky, weed-infested.

Gradually the form took a kind of familiar shape. He had seen a hull like that before. The spiky things pushing upwards were broken masts.

It was the skeleton of an old ship!

Excitement surged through him. He had found shipwreck territory!

6. Pirate Gold

There seemed to be hundreds of wrecks – or bits of them anyway. Max cruised round the broken masts, and surprised a couple of eel-like creatures, which burst from a shattered porthole. As he swam, the rotten wood, undisturbed for centuries, fell apart at the merest brush of his fins. His boy's curiosity was aroused. What had happened, years ago, to make all these ships sink? Perhaps there were pirate ships in this part of the ocean, preying on the big galleons bringing treasures from South America.

He could imagine the terrible sea battles as the galleons tried to save their ships and their cargoes.

Then he was all shark, feeling the vibrations of the fish around him, smelling them with his fine senses, smelling . . . flesh. Another predator had killed, not long ago, and left half a large flat fish in the wreck. Max darted towards it and tore at the remains. *And I don't like fish!* he thought. *Not even fish fingers!*

But the snack made his shark self want more. He cruised round the wrecks, looking for something to catch. There was plenty of small fry. The shoals swirled and corkscrewed in the water, trying to confuse him, but he wasn't interested. He wanted something big, something plump and tasty. He could smell warm-blooded animal somewhere. Perhaps a seal? He would rush at it and in seconds his huge jaws would seize the creature, tossing it from side to side to rip the flesh from its bones.

Max's mouth opened, showing his fearsome teeth. A squid, changing colour as it passed from a drift of green seaweed to a colony of red sea anemones, shot a panicky cloud of ink in Max's face and pulsed rapidly away.

As he cruised through the ribs of long sunken ships, he forgot his hunger and began to explore the remains. The cabins were small cubbyholes, reminding him of the pigeon holes his father kept his papers in. *They're not much larger!* he thought. *How did people manage to sleep in here, against the cannons and the stores? Perhaps they had larger rooms somewhere else?* But as he swam round the biggest wreck, exploring down the wooden steps and round the companionways, he could only find one real room. It was high up on the outer side of the ship, with windows that must at one time have looked out over the sea. *This must have been for the captain,* Max thought.

There was nothing much in the room. There was the top half of a chair, but the fabric had rotted and its wooden legs were so eaten by marine worms that the rest of it had crumbled to a mushy pile in the middle of the floor. He wondered why the rest of the ship was still there when everything in it, but the iron cannons, seemed to have gone. Then he remembered Uncle Herbert saying something about the ships being built of stout oak, which would resist rotting. Perhaps treasure hunters had already taken away anything interesting.

He saw a shadow of something that didn't dart away from him. It had separate fins on its tail, a huge round eye, and something in front of it, which seemed to be another big-eyed fish, swimming at the same speed. Was it being chased by the bigger fish?

His shark brain tried to puzzle it out. He could smell it. He knew that smell. A mixture of warm-blooded flesh and rubber. But was it good to eat? Was the rubbery smell some kind of blubber, a covering of fat to keep the animal warm?

There were more of them, their divided flippers lazily moving them round the wrecks. He wanted one. He wanted to sink his huge teeth into its flesh, and rip it apart . . .

They were scuba divers, treasure hunters, diving down to see what they could take from these ancient, wrecked ships. With a huge effort, Max once again resisted the shark urge to kill.

The diver pointed his camera excitedly and waved his hands to his companions. *Look at this brilliant shark*, he seemed to say, *I'm filming it! How cool is that!*

No, don't come anywhere near me! Max wanted to shout, but instead his jaws gaped and the diver hurtled back to a safe place behind the rusted cannon on the wreck's gun deck. The camera's eye

glared through a gun port, filming Max as he thrashed his tail to pilot himself in and out of the narrow spaces.

The diver with the camera flapped his finned feet and shot away into the belly of the ship, where Max had just been exploring. He wanted to tell the guy there was nothing there – nothing but old guns. No treasure. There was no point in looking any further. It had all been taken away years ago.

He wanted to tell the explorers what he'd seen,

to point out that this cabin was empty; that doorway held nothing. But they kept their distance. He couldn't blame them for being wary of him. He was a mighty big shark, after all!

Max flipped his tail and surged further downwards, away from the divers. He didn't want to frighten them. There were plenty of wrecks for them all to explore.

One ship was more deeply embedded than the others. Perhaps it was older — perhaps it had been the first of all these vessels to go down. It was covered in seaweed and barnacles, and Max only thought it might be a ship because of the curved shape sticking out of the mud. He flipped his tail and almost overshot it — it was nearer than he thought. In fact, the whole ship was much smaller than he thought. He bent his flexible body round and swam back more slowly. His movements stirred the murky waters into a thick vegetable soup, so he couldn't see anything clearly now at all. It was strange that there was very little sea life round here.

And then he saw some wriggly carving on the pointed end of the hull.

I need hands! he gasped to himself as he bumped and barged the wreck to try and clear off some of the frondy weeds. As he rubbed his body against it great mats of weed tore off like sticking plasters from a sore. His skin was so rough that it easily scraped away at the barnacles and green growth.

Soon he had cleared enough away for him to read the words carved on the prow.

... MALA NOC ...

The *Mala Noche*!

So Uncle Herbert really had been down here before him! How weird was that? Mum never told them he'd been a scuba diver! Excitedly, Max dived down into the murk and pushed his nose into the thick mud at the bottom.

Coins. Thousands of them! They didn't look like coins – more like furry pebbles – but as he rasped his rough skin against them the mud and weed fell off and he could begin to see the same design which was on Uncle Herbert's coin. They were doubloons – Spanish gold, that had lain undiscovered for hundreds of years!

The fishy part of him caught a movement. His body tensed, the muscles ready to attack.

Lying right on top of a broken casket was the biggest animal Max had ever seen! It was a dark red, rusty colour. A huge tentacle moved lazily, curling round the casket as if to protect it. The one eye that was showing was as big as a hubcap and it was looking straight at him.

It was a giant squid!

7. Billy the Squid

The giant creature watched Max, but did not move. Only its tentacles shifted lazily in the ocean currents. Who knew how long it had been lying there. Was this creature the reason no divers were exploring this wreck?

Max tried frantically to remember what his parents had told him and Molly about giant squid. For once, he wished he'd listened to them a bit more. Little bits of his mum's words came back to him. *It hunts small sea creatures, but larger animals feed on it.*

Was he a large enough animal to eat a giant squid? He hoped so. Not that he wanted to eat one, but better that than the other way round.

More of his mum's words came into his mind: *it grabs its prey with those long, long tentacles, then the squid's beak chops the victim up into bite-sized pieces . . .*

Max hoped, desperately, that the squid would think a Galapagos shark was too big to tackle for its supper.

It certainly didn't look scared of him.

Then he remembered some more. He could see his dad's face grow intense as he told the twins about this rare and beautiful creature that lived in the depths of the ocean where few other creatures even ventured. *They're not harmful unless you provoke them.*

Yeah, but that's people, said Max to himself. *I'm not a person at the moment.*

He decided to believe his dad and leave the

squid alone, hoping the animal wouldn't wind an armful of suckers round him just when he thought he was safe.

Max really wanted to have a good look at the *Mala Noche* while he was here, so that he could tell Uncle Herbert all about it. There was no way he could pick up a gold coin to prove he'd found the ship, but he could tell his uncle how he'd swum through all the rooms and seen something of how the pirates of so long ago must have lived.

Max drifted through the hull, trying to understand what he could see. So much had sunk into the mud, or wedged into cracks in the coral, it was difficult to work out where everything had once been. It looked as if the ship had ended up lying on its side in the ooze. There were cannons, like on the other ships, one of them still pointing out of what had been a porthole. It was pointing up to the surface.

He flicked his tail sharply and the movement of the water pushed away another load of thick mud. Under the mud his sharp shark eyes saw a beautiful round instrument made of brass – or what Max thought must be brass. He could see a dull gleam even through the film of mud. *Perhaps that's how they navigated*, he thought. *I bet the divers would have been pleased to see that. Perhaps when Billy the Squid moves away people will come back and collect some of these old things from the* Mala Noche.

As he thrust his way through the corridors, past the rotting wood of cabins, he saw a smaller squid shoot into a porthole. Max-the-shark made a dart for it. His mouth wanted to tear at its flesh, like Max-the-boy would want to lick an ice cream. What did it matter if he normally hated seafood? He was hungry.

No! his boy-brain screamed. He couldn't kill this creature! His head snapped round, his fearsome

teeth grazing the floor of a deck. They came in contact with something hard; something sharp flew into his nose, cutting through its tough skin.

Harpoon! The warning signals flashed into his brain from both the fish side and the human side. But his instinct was wrong. When he saw what it really was, he tried to laugh, but the muscles of his face wouldn't do what he wanted them to do. He had crashed into a chest, breaking through the wood. But the metal band which held it together had sprung upwards, its sharp edge cutting into him.

Even in the murk, Max could see there were fabulous jewels here. There must have been something else as well — perhaps bales of silk? — because he knew the treasure galleons carried other valuables, besides gold and silver. Whatever it was, it had turned to sludge, and now the moving water was washing it away.

Why was there moving water? Max whipped round. He was picking up vibrations along the lateral lines that ran the length of his shark body. It was weird the way he could detect creatures' movements through vibrations in the water. He hadn't felt the giant squid because it was so still. But now vibrations were coming thick and fast. A shoal of fish? It felt different from the shoals he'd met before, and there was no fishy scent.

Max could smell warm, human blood again. Remembering his hunger, he was suddenly filled with an urge to hunt those humans down and sink his teeth into their flesh . . .

No! Max screamed silently to himself. *I'm human – I can't!*

There were more of the divers now. Their powerful torches flashed this way and that as they looked for him. They must have followed him and noticed the treasure that he'd uncovered. Even though they could see an enormous Galapagos shark guarding it, they must have decided to risk an attack to get to the treasure.

There were more than enough divers to outwit a shark. They had a harpoon, too. And one of the divers was aiming it straight at Max.

He had a split second to decide what to do. His shark instincts told him to rush at the divers and attack. He knew the ocean, he had the speed, he had a whiplash body.

And he had the teeth. Rows and rows of teeth.

His jaws gaped open, ready to rush at the divers. His human mind knew how they would attack; it knew how he could avoid being pierced by the harpoon. His shark mind knew how to stir up the murky seabed to create a dense cloud. When their sight was fogged he would feel their presence and be able to attack. With both the animal and the human parts of his brain, he could easily overpower the treasure hunters: he could easily kill them.

Max darted into the *Mala Noche*. The divers followed, but quickly spotted the giant squid and didn't want to disturb it.

Max didn't want to disturb it either. He was still not sure whether it would attack him if he made a commotion. Besides, it was a legend. Hardly anyone had ever seen a giant squid alive. His parents would be really excited if they knew it was here. He wanted it to stay there, where it belonged.

Max sped through the ship to the stern, curling in and out of the fragile ribs, dodging bulkheads, winding his flexible body round the great wooden posts, which used to divide the different parts of the ship. He could feel the human divers trying to follow him.

He could so easily turn on them and destroy them. But they were people, and not bad people either. They were just exploring, and he *was* a very impressive-looking shark, after all.

Suddenly, Max felt his huge bulk working against him. There was no room for him to move and dodge the divers. He swam deeper and deeper into the body of the ship, trying to find a way out.

He was trapped!

8. A Tight Corner

In panic, Max jack-knifed backwards and forwards, trying to evade the diver with the harpoon. Then he shot forwards into what looked like an opening in the ship. Wrong! What he thought was a way out was in fact a staircase down into the bottom of the ship. He saw heaps of round things – the shot for the cannons! But the further he swam, the narrower the space became, until his huge body was nearly wedged between the cannon balls and the great timbers of the keel.

Through his lateral lines, Max could feel the divers coming nearer and nearer. Frightened, he bounced his head against the side of the ship. Perhaps the wood was fragile enough to crash his way through? His shark eyes could see through the swirling mud. They weren't very near – yet. He thrashed his tail to stir up more sludge. At least he would be able to see them coming, and they wouldn't be able to see him.

But he was still trapped!

Torches flickered, making cloudy tunnels in the murky water.

Then in one of the torch flashes Max's sharp, shark eyes could see a different colour in the stout sides of the ship. A darker hole. Perhaps a cannonball hole – the reason why the *Mala Noche* had sunk?

He made for it, and pushed his snout into the opening.

No! It might be big enough to sink the ship, but it wasn't quite big enough for a shark.

Got to get out! Max thought. *But I can't swim backwards and there isn't room to turn!*

There was only one thing to do.

Desperately, he shoved his fins against the wooden sides of the ship, edging back inch by inch. The divers were close. He could see the excited waving of their torches. It was crazy to go back towards them, but he couldn't stay where he was. He seized his chance.

Just as the divers were practically on to him, Max barrelled his way forwards with a powerful thrust of his tail, and burst through the side of the ship, sending rotten wood splintering slowly through the water like dandelion parachutes on dry land.

Pleased with himself, Max shot up towards the clearer waters near the surface. He charged through a shoal of astonished blue and yellow angelfish, scattering them like coloured sweets at a party.

A school of yellowfin tuna nervously swerved and grouped round a passing pod of dolphins.

Funny, thought Max. *I don't feel interested in dolphins. How weird is that? Perhaps they don't taste good?*

He grinned a shark grin as the silvery tuna shoaled round the dolphins. It was great to be king of the ocean again. A huge school of jacks, hunting for their own food, saw Max and rushed off in a cloud. And then there was another shoal of tuna, this time without their protective dolphins. In fact, the whole sea seemed to be thick with tuna! One of the reasons why the twins' parents had been so keen to come to Malpelo Island because tuna are protected here. Nobody is allowed to fish for them.

'But they're not protected from me!' sniggered Max as he chased a red snapper through a bright purple and yellow coral reef.

Suddenly, Max's terrible shark hunger threatened to overcome him and he swerved away from the snapper before his great teeth moved in for the kill.

Something unfamiliar drifted past his nose, and a shadow passed overhead. He realised what the strange thing was only just in time. It was a net. A fishing net. It stretched for several metres under the water and already there were several fish trapped in it. The shadow overhead must be a fishing boat.

But the fish are supposed to be protected! gasped Max. *And anyway, they shouldn't be fishing with nets!* Even where the fish were not protected, you were only supposed to catch them by hook and line. The drift nets catch too many fish, and sometimes dolphins get tangled up in them too.

Max surged up to the surface and began to circle the boat, hoping that his threatening dorsal fin would frighten the fishermen away. Or perhaps he could ram the boat, and try to make it rock so much that the shouting fishermen would fall in.

They were frightened, but fear of the shark wasn't going to make them go away. Someone had grabbed a huge spear and was aiming it at Max. He dived down again, wondering whether to shove at the boat from the bottom.

Then his sharp shark's hearing picked up a high-pitched squeaking. It was the same noise the dolphin playing with Molly had made earlier. The noise it had made when Slynk's dart had pierced its side.

Max dropped back down in the water, and found a dolphin entangled in the fine nylon threads of the drift net.

It looked terrified as Max approached it. Sharks might keep away when dolphins are swimming freely, but this one was captive, unable to escape from those huge jaws. Yet it kept on crying out, as if it was asking Max to help it.

He had to do something! He couldn't let the dolphin be caught and speared by those men up on the boat. But what could he do? He didn't have any hands to untangle it!

Then he remembered his jaws. If they could bite through fish bones they would have no problem tearing through a bit of nylon netting!

Swiftly he went to work, turning his head to the side so that the jaws under his nose could get at the strands of the net. As he worked he could see a scar on the dolphin's side – it was from a recent wound. He'd seen that scar before!

You're the dolphin Professor Slynk shot with his horrible little robot dart! he exclaimed to himself. And

he gnawed even harder at the netting to try and release it.

The dolphin shrieked louder as Max's jaws came closer.

Max wanted to reassure it, but he didn't know dolphin language, and besides, he couldn't make the whistles and clicks that dolphins make.

At last the dolphin was free. It darted away, but in a few seconds it came back, chirping at Max.

It seemed to be saying thank you!

You're welcome, thought Max. But the dolphin had gone.

He had been in the ocean for a long time. He didn't know where he was. It was time he found out where Slynk's yacht was and made his way back to it, before he began to transform back into a boy.

He turned to swim away from the boat and the net, and wondered why it seemed so difficult. The boat and the net seemed to be coming with him.

And then he realised. He wasn't swimming at all. He could feel the drift net round his tail.

It was stuck. He was caught in an illegal fishing net!

9. Netted!

Max thrashed his tail, trying to whip it round and out of the snares.

It was no use. He was still stuck.

This is mad, thought Max. *I'm one of the most powerful creatures in the sea. I just can't be caught in a stupid fishing net!*

He twisted round, but his tail wouldn't twist with him. He tried to jump, but he couldn't even get his nose above the water. The net jumped with him and caught one of his fins as he came down.

A blue and yellow spiny lobster fanned its tail past him. Max snapped at it crossly, but his jaws couldn't get anywhere near the creature. A large puffer fish swelled up with fright, its spines ready to stick into the thrashing shark.

Oh, don't be so silly! Max wanted to tell it. *Can't you see there's no way I can get at you? Yet*, he added. Only a matter of time and he'd be out of the net and scorching back to Slynk's yacht.

Bi-colour parrot fish and a small shoal of yellow canary blennies swam past, swirling in Max's thrashing whirlpools. They swam right through the drift-net holes.

All right for you! thought Max, snarling, his jaws gaping so that they scurried away. *When I get out of here I'll have you for dinner!*

But his shark appetite had gone completely. He needed all his energy to haul himself out of his prison. He had to calm down and work it out.

OK, he said to himself, *I bit a way out for the dolphin. I can definitely bite a way out for myself.* He knew his flexible back would fold almost in half. He could bring his head round – like *that* – and tear at the netting with his razor-sharp teeth.

But he couldn't quite get there. His nose got in the way. His teeth were underneath, and even when he gaped his jaws as wide as they would go, he couldn't manage to get at the nylon threads.

He tried to whip his head back again, but it wouldn't turn. The fin on his right side was caught now.

In panic, he twisted and turned, jack-knifed and nearly folded himself in half, but he couldn't untangle himself. The more he thrashed about, the more tangled he became, and now he was so caught up that he couldn't get his jaws anywhere near the net that trapped him.

He hung like a fly caught in a spider's web, as fish cruised past.

Then the worst happened.

He began to feel the tingle in his body that meant he was about to transform back into a boy.

'Nooo!' he shrieked, and bubbles flew from his mouth. Unlike him, however, they escaped. He began to panic again. If he changed now he wouldn't be able to breathe underwater. He would die in minutes! He wouldn't even be able to swim to the surface. And even if he could, how far was he from the yacht? Would he ever find it again?

He thrashed his body back and forth, creating great swirls of current and sending the little fish flying through the water in alarm.

It was no good. It looked as though he was doomed to a watery grave, just like the sailors of those wrecked ships down on the ocean floor.

His head was buzzing. It was panic. Sheer panic.

OK, Max, he told himself, *calm down and think about this*.

That was easier said than done. Every time he moved he could feel the net ensnaring him, and he had another panic and another thrash about, getting himself even more tangled.

What's the point of having the best teeth in the ocean if I can't use them! he thought.

If he transformed back under water he would have to hold his breath and try to undo the net with his fingers. If he took too long he'd run out of breath!

His tail began to divide. It felt as if it was being ripped apart.

Nooo, thought Max. His toes wriggled. It was all wrong this way round! He *needed* that tail, to power himself away when he'd untangled the net. And he needed his fingers, not his toes!

His skin was shrinking painfully as it tried to cover the huge shark muscles, then his insides unfolded and folded again into human guts. He was changing back too quickly. He had to think even faster. His fins opened, slit, and began to turn into hands.

He pulled frantically at the net. But the nylon was too strong, he couldn't break it.

But he still had his shark head and jaws. And he could bend right over, close to where his legs were caught. In the split second before his shark head changed back into that of a boy, he turned it into a biting position and tore at the net. His teeth cut through it like swords. The last of the threads severed, and there was a hole in the net, just big enough for him to swim through.

Hey, didn't know I could swim like this! Max thought, pleased with himself. He could still move like a fish in the water, and some of the oxygen his fishy gills had pumped into his blood was keeping his human body alive.

His head popped out of the water like a cork. He was safe!

Or was he?

He was the only person in the whole of the ocean. There were no boats, nothing but the sea birds and the black, jutting rocky outline of Malpelo Island. Which was a long, long way away.

Max was a pretty good swimmer, but the extra power he'd had as a shark was now draining away.

He looked across the heaving water to the island. One of its mountains looked just like a shark fin.

Even if he was strong enough to swim all the way to the yacht, there was no guarantee he'd get back alive. There were still sharks in the ocean. In fact, what had his parents been looking at? Shoals of hammerheads?

He shivered in the water. When he had been a shark he had seen hundreds of things that might like to take a bite out of a boy. The fact that he couldn't see them now didn't make them any less dangerous!

Max saw something plop out of the water not too far from him. A heaving, shining back.

He might have escaped the net, but if that was a shark, he was doomed. One way or another, it looked as if he was going to die in the ocean!

10. Home and Dry

The heaving back leapt again. He could see a fin cut the water and he screamed.

Then the animal leapt right out of the ocean, and Max could see the friendly face of a bottlenose dolphin.

He sighed with relief. It wasn't a shark after all!

But that still wouldn't help him get back to the yacht any faster. He was going to have to swim for it. And it was *miles!*

The dolphin leapt again. It seemed to be on its

own. Max trod water for a while to watch it. No point wearing himself out straight away. He knew dolphins swam in the wake of boats, to help them get more speed. Perhaps they swam with the current as well. If he watched this animal, and watched the odd bits of weed on the surface of the water, he might see which way the current was flowing and hope it was in the right direction. Then he could either drift with the current or be helped by it.

There was a rapid clicking noise. It was the dolphin.

Must be talking to its friends, thought Max. *I wonder what it's saying?*

The dolphin clicked again, more urgently. It swam right up to Max and shoved itself against him.

'Oh, hi,' said Max nervously. 'Um — I'm just, er, hanging around . . .' He felt a bit silly, talking to a dolphin. Good thing Molly wasn't with him or she'd make one of her sarcastic comments.

Impatiently the dolphin pushed him again, then rolled over so that Max could see its side.

'You've been hurt.' He remembered his father telling him how dolphin skin was smooth and quite soft, to give them speed in the water, but this meant they got scarred by attacks from predators or even from their own kind when mock-fighting during the mating season. 'Did a shark get you?'

The dolphin whistled, as if he was being very silly. It did a complete roll, and showed him the injury again. The wound was fresh; it was still oozing blood.

'I am so thick!' shouted Max. 'It's you again, isn't it? That was where Professor Stink hit you with the robot dart! Yeah – sorry. But you know it wasn't me, don't you?' Max wondered whether the dolphin recognised him as the shark who'd rescued it shortly before.

The dolphin rolled again, then leaped out of the sea, darting in a series of jumps into the distance.

'Yeah, well, I'm glad you know it wasn't me, or Molly,' he said sadly to himself. 'But I wish you'd stayed around. If I'm going to drown, it would be nice to have company.'

The dolphin came back in a rush, and shoved itself right against him, leaning over so that its

dorsal fin tickled Max's chest.

'Do you want to play?' said Max. 'It's OK, but I really need to keep my strength . . .'

The dolphin whistled and clicked, and shoved its dorsal fin right into Max's face, as if he was being very stupid.

Which he was.

'Oh, I get you!' he breathed. 'Thanks, dolphin!'

He grabbed hold of the fin, and with an approving whistle the dolphin moved off through the water, pulling Max alongside it.

It was quite difficult to grip, but the dolphin seemed to realise this and was careful not to swim too fast. Even so, Max's arms were aching and, with the spray exploding into his face, his eyes were blurred by the time they got near to the island.

The dolphin seemed to know it was unwise to get too close – it had been attacked by humans on that yacht before. As Max gratefully let go, it gave another series of rapid clicks and disappeared under the sea.

'Max! Here!'

It was Molly's urgent voice.

He could see his parents leaning over the rail. There was no sign of Slynk. Molly was leaning over the little rope ladder she had used to climb up from her swim, waving his swimming trunks. He grabbed her hand and hauled himself out of the water.

'It was brilliant,' he told her as he dried off in his cabin. His hands reached out to his computer console, but somehow the adventures of *Ecco the Dolphin* didn't seem quite as interesting now that he'd experienced the real thing. 'Well, most of it was. Until I got stuck in a fishing net.'

'You didn't?' shrieked Molly. 'You stupid idiot!'

'Yeah, well, I was rescuing a dolphin,' said Max modestly, 'and I kind of got caught up afterwards.'

'Anyway, what was a net doing there?' said Molly. 'Nobody's supposed to fish round here. The tuna are protected.'

'Exactly,' said Max. 'I did try to scare the fishermen off, but I bet they'll be back as soon as it's dark. We'd better tell Mum and Dad and get them stopped.'

'Oh, yeah – and how did we see them?' said Molly sarcastically. 'Like they're just over there, in broad daylight?'

'We – we saw them through our telescope?' suggested Max. He saw Molly's doubtful face and said hurriedly, 'I know, it's a bit of a long shot, but you know Mum and Dad. They'll be so worried about the tuna getting caught they won't even think about *how* we saw them.'

'What else?' said Molly. 'It's not fair, you getting all these adventures and me being stuck on this boat with Slynk.'

'Oh, yeah, and I had to fight off these divers and nearly got stuck in a wreck.' He told Molly about the treasure and the giant squid protecting it. 'I fought it off single-finned,' he began, then he saw Molly's face. 'OK, so I didn't,' he grinned. 'I just left it alone and it left me alone. I wish Professor Stink had been down there – it would be cool to scare him off for ever!'

'No chance,' said Molly. 'You mean, there really are wrecks down there? I asked one of the crew about Uncle Herbert's treasure ship, but they said it was a legend and had never been found. They've explored all the old wrecks there already and there's nothing in them, they said. I knew Uncle was talking rubbish!'

Slowly Max pulled Uncle Herbert's coin out of

his pocket and looked at it, gleaming on the palm of his hand.

'Uncle Herbert gave it to me,' Max explained. 'I saw coins just like it on the ocean bed.' Max paused. He wasn't sure she would believe him. 'Molly, I saw it. I saw the *Mala Noche*.'

'Wow,' said Molly. She took the coin. 'Looks like real treasure,' she admitted, 'but how did Uncle Herbert get hold of it?'

'Uncle Herbert said he'd explored the *Mala Noche* when he was young.'

'I don't believe it. I bet he nicked the coin from a museum or something. Can you see him finding his way down to a wreck that nobody else can locate? And then finding his way out again?'

Max laughed too. 'Specially when he even gets lost in the supermarket,' he agreed. 'But if he'd never been, how did he know where the *Mala Noche* was?'

'Beats me,' Molly shrugged.

Max shut his eyes and imagined himself cruising round the wreck, sending shoals of fish scuttling in fear. That was cool, but it had been even better just being underwater, being able to swim effortlessly through the amazing coral reefs. 'Yeah,' he said almost to himself. 'It was great. Even though it was a bit scary at times.'

'Well, next time you'd better do what Brain Strain says and turn into a sea sponge – much safer!' said Molly crossly.

Safer, yes. But Max was gradually changing from the lazy, junk food-eating boy he used to be. The dangers were real, but so was the excitement.

Still, he'd had enough excitement for the time being. All he wanted to do now was put his feet up and watch the sea from the safety of his cabin window.

More Stupendous Shark Facts!

They're older than your gran! Sharks have lived on this planet for almost 400 million years and they can live to be 100 years old!

They're speedy! Most sharks whiz along at between 30 and 60 kilometres per hour. One shark – the mako shark – has been known to go at speeds of up to 95 kilometres per hour!

They have loads of babies! Most sharks have 6 to 12 babies at any one time. The hammerhead and tiger sharks, however, can have as many as 40 at once!

They're all shapes and sizes! The smallest shark is the spined pygmy shark, which is only 17 to 20 centimetres long. The biggest shark is the whale shark that grows up to 14 metres long!

They're not as dangerous as wasps! Experts think that most shark attacks on humans are mistakes, and happen when sharks taste humans to see if they're worth eating, or when the big fish mistake scuba-divers or surfers (in their dark wetsuits) for seals or sea lions.

They've got super-senses! Sharks can feel vibrations in the water using canals called 'lateral lines' that run the length of their bodies. These are filled with water and have sensory cells with hairs growing out of them. The hairs move when the water vibrates so the shark knows when something good to eat swims by.

ONLY JOKING!

What's a shark's favourite game?

Swallow the leader!

Whats green and gross and lives under the sea?

Shark bogeys!

Why did the shark cross the road?

To get to the other tide!

What does a shark eat for dinner?

Whatever it wants!

What happens when you cross a shark with a cow?

I don't know, but I wouldnt want to milk it!

What do you call a shark in a red-and-white furry hat?

Santa Jaws!

Why don't sharks eat clowns?

Because they taste funny!

What time was the shark's appointment with the dentist?

Tooth-hurty!

Are You Super-Sharp on Movie Sharks?

1. The Sharks were a gang in which old film?

A *West Side Story*

B *Flipper*

C *Mary Poppins*

2. Jaws, the most famous movie shark ever, is pretty hefty, but the heaviest whale shark ever accurately recorded weighed:

A 210 kilograms

B 2,100 kilograms

C 21,000 kilograms

3. Was there a shark in the Disney movie *The Little Mermaid?*

A No – Mr Disney wouldn't want to scare the little kiddies!

B Yes, one – a very nasty piece of work

C Yes, two charming sharks actually

Sharpen up your shark knowledge with this movie-based quiz!

4. Which of the following films would a shark fan most enjoy?

A *Babe*

B *Monsters Inc.*

C *Shark Tale*

5. Which of the following films doesn't feature sharks?

A *Cars*

B *Finding Nemo*

C *Jaws*

Are you blunt as a butter knife or sharper than a great white's gnashers? Check the answers and find out!

1 = A   2 = C   3 = B   4 = C   5 = A

UNCLE HERBERT'S SHARK SUB

We asked Uncle Herbert to scrap his version of this recipe (containing actual shark meat), and went with this vegetarian one instead. Frighten your friends (or just make them crack up laughing), or pop one in your lunchbox and give the dinner ladies a scare!

YOU'LL NEED:

A long, soft bread roll

A packet of sliced cheese

A pitted black olive, halved

A jar of mayonnaise or pickle

A grown-up helper

HERE'S WHAT TO DO:

1 Ask your grown-up to cut the roll open lengthways

2 Spread a thin layer of mayonnaise or pickle all over the inside

3 Lay two cheese slices on top of the mayonnaise or pickle and press the sandwich together

4 Take another two cheese slices. Get your adult to help you cut out:
   - One tail shape
   - Three fin shapes
   - Some pointy teeth

5 'Glue' the fins and teeth into place using the sticky mayonnaise or pickle (see photo)

6 Finish by pressing on the olive 'eyes'

7 Eat!

YUM!

Can't wait for the next book
in the series?
Here's a sneak preview of

SNAKE SCARE

1. Going to the Zoo, Zoo, Zoo

The kitchen door crashed open, then was slammed shut with such force that Uncle Herbert's pictures swayed crookedly on their hooks.

'That's the *fifth* time he's been round the garden,' Molly exclaimed angrily. 'Even Professor Stink can't pretend he's here to watch the May blossom come out!'

Her twin brother Max joined her as she glared out of the kitchen window at a strange, scruffy creature, which seemed to be jumping from tree to tree in Uncle Herbert's big untidy garden.

'I know he's thick, but doesn't he realise people put scarecrows in fields, not gardens?' marvelled Max. 'That's the worst disguise yet. I'm going to start listing them and giving them marks out of ten.'

He sounded jokey but underneath he was deeply worried. Professor Preston Slynk – a zoologist, like the twins' parents – was desperate to find out how Max transformed into animals and would stop at nothing to be able to grab Max and take him to his private laboratory for tests.

'No point asking Uncle Herbert to get rid of him. He just wouldn't see the point,' gloomed Max.

'He just wouldn't *see* him,' added Molly. 'Even if he had three heads!'

Max felt suddenly cheerful at the vision of Slynk with three heads. He began happily drawing a picture of him in the margin of his geography homework with one hand, while shovelling down

a bowl of cornflakes with the other.

Molly stopped in her tracks. 'You're doing homework! Are you feeling all right? I thought you'd got a new computer game. I've never heard of *anyone* doing geography at breakfast time, specially you!'

'I forgot about it last week. Mr Miller said if I didn't give it in when I got to school, I wouldn't be able to go on the zoo trip,' he explained.

'Bor-*ing*,' said Molly. 'Anyway, I thought you didn't want anything to do with animals if you didn't have to.' It was bad enough, Max usually reasoned, to have to travel to various animal-packed countries around the world during the holidays, without having to see animals in school time, too.

Max's brow furrowed and he stabbed his geography homework with his biro. 'I want to know what makes my animal transformations happen,' he said. 'Is it because I'm thinking about it, or do I have to touch it, or what?'

'Can't be touching it,' said Molly. 'You didn't touch a mouse yesterday.' She grinned. 'Ahhh, you did look sweet!'

'You were just like Stink, trying to make me do tricks,' said Max furiously.

'I was *not*!' screeched Molly. She kick-boxed the

underneath of the table so that his homework flew into the air then landed in a messy heap on the floor.

Max shrugged. He wasn't enjoying the geography anyway. 'Hey, yesterday I slipped through a hole in the floorboards and found another of Uncle Herbert's secret rooms. If Stink manages to invade the house we can always hide in there.'

'If we can find the human way in,' said Molly gloomily. 'I couldn't squeeze into a tiny hole in the floorboards.'

Max had to admit he couldn't either, not while he was a boy anyway. But he'd really enjoyed looking at – and sometimes nibbling – all Uncle Herbert's mysterious objects stored in the attic and basement. 'I wonder where he got all that stuff from? What a pity I changed back just as Jake got here.' Molly had phoned his friend as soon as Max had transformed into a mouse, but Jake arrived too late to see more than a heap of mouse droppings.

Molly changed the subject. 'You can't go transforming at the zoo,' she instructed. 'What if Slynk follows you and grabs you?'

'He won't be there today,' boasted Max. 'And how would he know I was going on a trip?' Max grabbed a couple of slices of bread and began spreading peanut butter rapidly over them. 'Chuck over a couple of packets of crisps will you?'

'You may be ten minutes older than me,' retorted Molly, 'but I'm not your servant. Get them yourself.'

'Anyway, I'll have Jake with me when I transform,' went on Max. 'He'll cover for me.' He opened the fridge and eyed its contents. There was a dish of spaghetti with pink custard sauce over it (Uncle Herbert had made it for tea last night – there was rather a lot left), an open tin of sardines, some stale slices of cheese and a bag of green chillis. His hand hovered over the sardines, then came down on the chillis and a couple of slices of the cheese. 'So I'll be quite safe,' he finished. He found a knife on the draining board and began to carefully chop the chillis, scattering them over the peanut butter, then slapping the slices together.

'You can't eat peanut butter with chillis!' shrilled Molly.

'Why not?' said Max.

'Because . . . because . . .' Molly sighed. 'Changing into animals has changed *you* into a weirdo. What on earth will you turn into next?'

'A toothless squirrel,' beamed Uncle Herbert.

The children turned and gasped in horror. Molly had forgotten to keep her voice down when they were talking about her brother's transformations. How long had Uncle Herbert been standing there?

'Wh-what?' stammered Max.

'A toothless squirrel,' twinkled their uncle. 'Oh, sorry – I've done it wrong – that's the *answer*! What animal uses a nutcracker? That's what I should have said. I must get my riddles the right way round.'

He turned and shuffled out, muttering to himself as he went.

'That was close!' breathed Molly. 'Better not talk about zoos any more, just in case.'

'Suits me,' said Max, cross with Molly for always telling him what to do. He slid some of the stale cheese into his sandwich when she wasn't looking. He didn't want her going on about his strange diet again.

'I wish *we* were going to the zoo,' moaned Samreen.

As usual, the twins had called for their best friends on their way to school.

'Tell you what, we'll do something else instead,' said Molly.

The two girls bent their heads together and giggled their way along the road.

'Do you reckon you might transform at the zoo?' whispered Jake. He was the only one of the twins' friends who knew about Max's strange ability, though he still wasn't sure whether to believe it or not. 'How did you change into that mouse yesterday? Do you have to think your way into it? Or trip over a pile of poo or something?'

'I didn't think about mice yesterday,' said Max. 'I was thinking about *Space Ninjas* and doing my homework . . . Oh, no! I've done it and I haven't brought it with me!' He emptied the contents of his bag out all over the pavement.

'Oh, yes, I have.' He sighed with relief and grinned at Jake.

As he repacked his bag, Max saw something out of the corner of his eye. Well, not something — someone. It was an old lady with a walking frame. A really gross old lady, with wiry grey hair sticking out of her headscarf, and monster warts all over her chin.

'Look out,' he giggled, 'there's an old witch behind us!'

The old lady was covering the ground very fast, even with the help of her walking frame. Surely she couldn't be . . .

He had to give Slynk top marks this time — if it hadn't been for the super-speedy walk, he really would have been fooled!